Farting Four-Toed Troll

Christmas Troll

By Lavelle Carlson

The Farting Four-toed Troll

Copyright 2019

Written by Lavelle Carlson
Illustrated by Donna Day Mathis
All Rights Reserved.

First Edition

ISBN: 978-0-578-60000-0
ISBN1O: 0-578-60000-5

This book is dedicated to my husband and my two daughters, Liana and Lisa who have given me five beautiful grandchildren, Taya Moore, Niko Moore, Emory Wardlaw, Rhodes Wardlaw, and Leni Wardlaw. My daughters grew up in Stavanger, Norway where their childhood was filled with stories of trolls. This book is also dedicated to all the wonderful children with whom I worked for many years as a speech/language pathologist.

This story is a fun take on the Christmas troll in Norway. In Norway he is called Jule Nissen (pronounced "you-le-neesan"). Traditionally, he feeds the animals at Christmas (Jule). However, this fun story gives a funny reason for how he came to do this. The story also teaches that it is best to call someone by their proper name (Jule Nissen or Christmas troll) and to say, "Excuse me" when necessary.

Before reading the story introduce the title and author. Ask the children what they think the troll should be named; Farting Four-Toed Troll or Christmas Troll or Jule Nissen as the children in Norway call him. The Jule Nissen is the Norwegian Christmas gnome or troll. Then say, "Let's read the book to see what is best to call him and why we should call him by that name.

After completing the story is a good time to discuss "good" words vs. "bad" words. What words make a person feel bad and what words make a person feel good?

Disclaimer:
The author of this book took "literary license" with this story and did not differentiate between trolls and nissen. This book is intended to be a short funny take on the Scandinavian mythology while teaching a lesson of kindness to animals as well as kindness to people (calling people by proper name). The author hopes that this book and other books on varying cultures will inspire children to learn about other peoples and cultures.

For those wanting to learn the mythological difference between trolls, nissen, and tomten I recommend the information on the link: http://trollmother.com/index.php/trollhistory. It states that, "The Nissen is a troll who lived on the farm and brought good luck to kind farm people." He also was kind and taught kindness. The trolls are often considered stubborn and mean. But, there can be many characteristics depending on the troll. Then, there is the Tomte that is similar to the troll but has a kinder face.

One of my favorite books (first published in 1962) is *A Time for Trolls, Fairy Tales from Norway* (as told by Asbjørnsen and Moe).

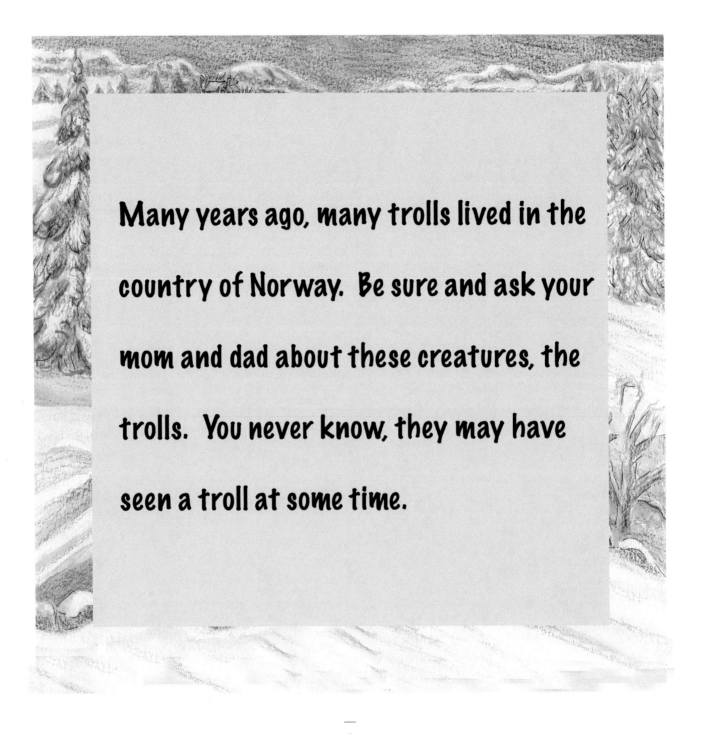

Many years ago, many trolls lived in the country of Norway. Be sure and ask your mom and dad about these creatures, the trolls. You never know, they may have seen a troll at some time.

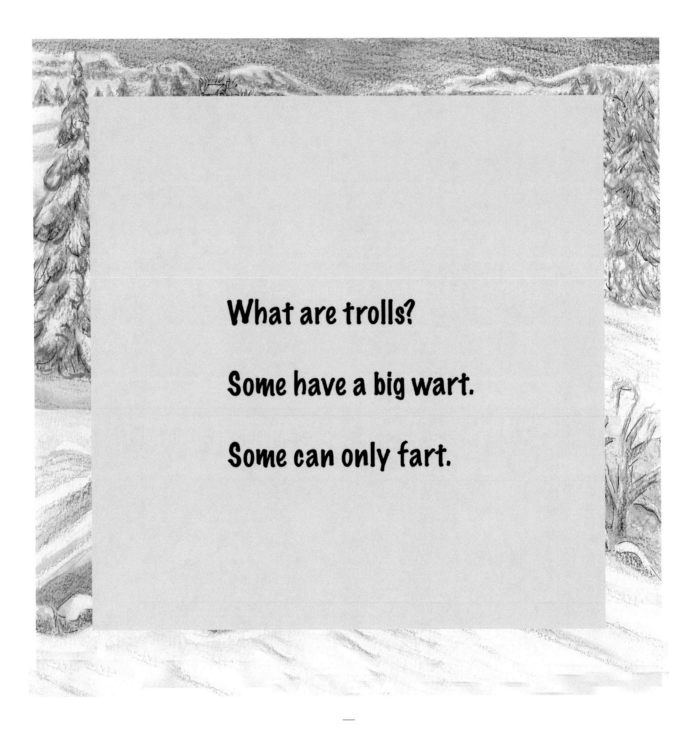

What are trolls?

Some have a big wart.

Some can only fart.

Then they say, "Excuse me".

Some are short.

They can only snort.

Some are fat.

They will only eat a fat rat.

Some are bad.

They get very mad.

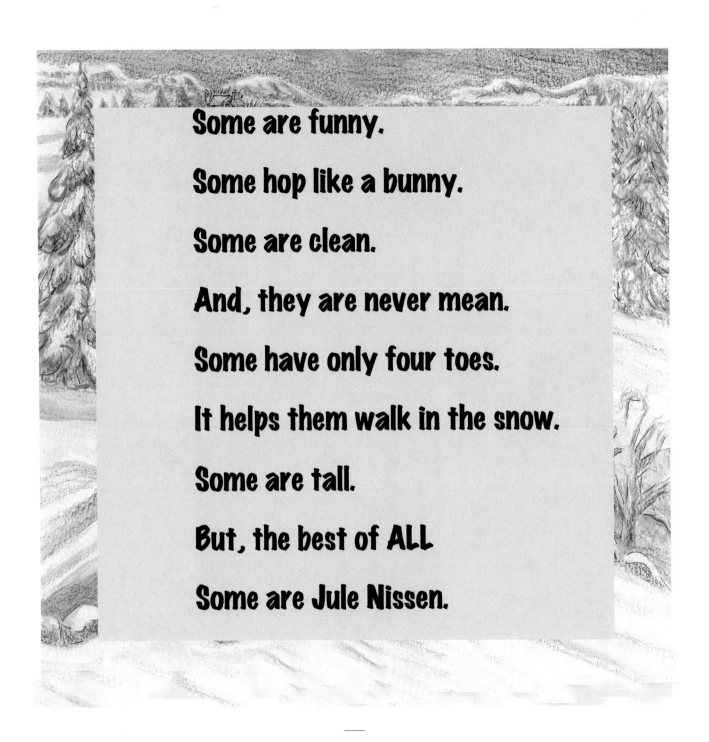

Some are funny.

Some hop like a bunny.

Some are clean.

And, they are never mean.

Some have only four toes.

It helps them walk in the snow.

Some are tall.

But, the best of ALL

Some are Jule Nissen.

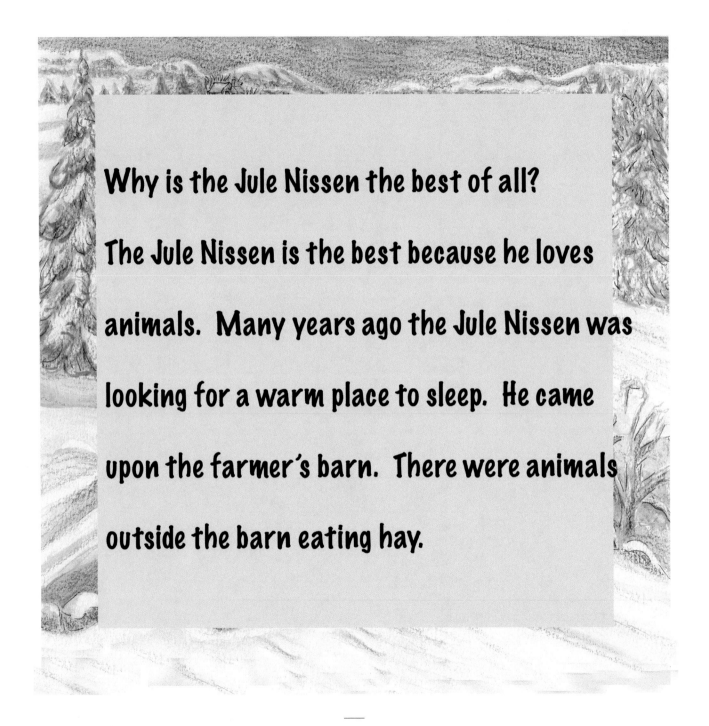

Why is the Jule Nissen the best of all?

The Jule Nissen is the best because he loves

animals. Many years ago the Jule Nissen was

looking for a warm place to sleep. He came

upon the farmer's barn. There were animals

outside the barn eating hay.

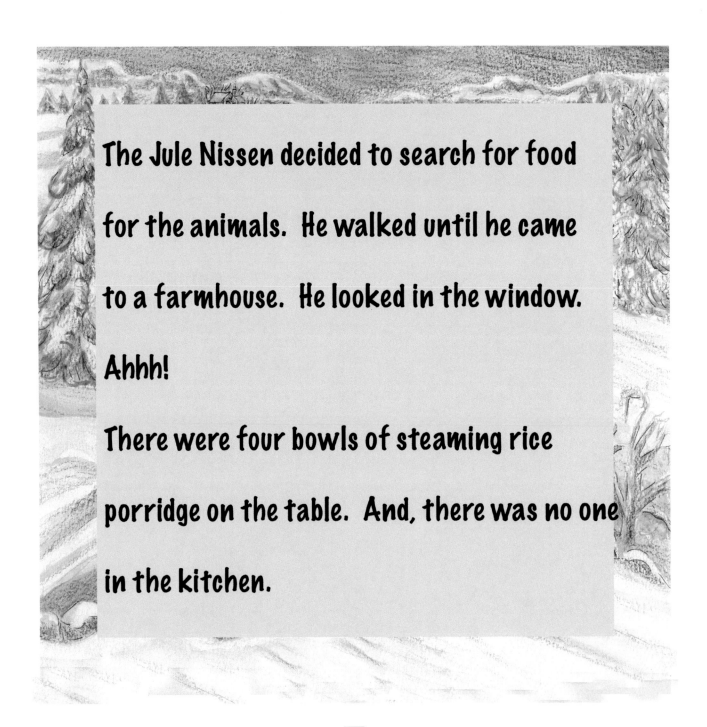

The Jule Nissen decided to search for food for the animals. He walked until he came to a farmhouse. He looked in the window.

Ahhh!

There were four bowls of steaming rice porridge on the table. And, there was no one in the kitchen.

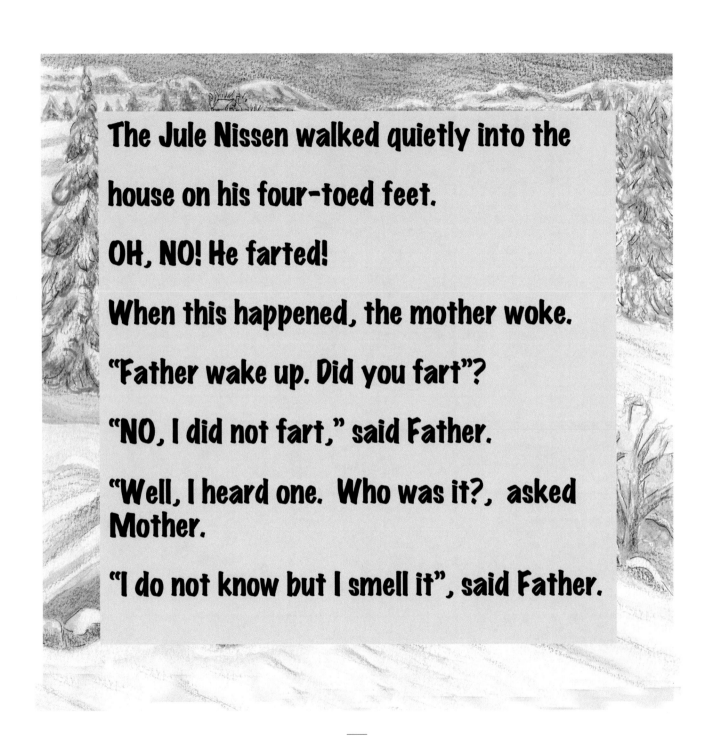

The Jule Nissen walked quietly into the house on his four-toed feet.

OH, NO! He farted!

When this happened, the mother woke.

"Father wake up. Did you fart"?

"NO, I did not fart," said Father.

"Well, I heard one. Who was it?, asked Mother.

"I do not know but I smell it", said Father.

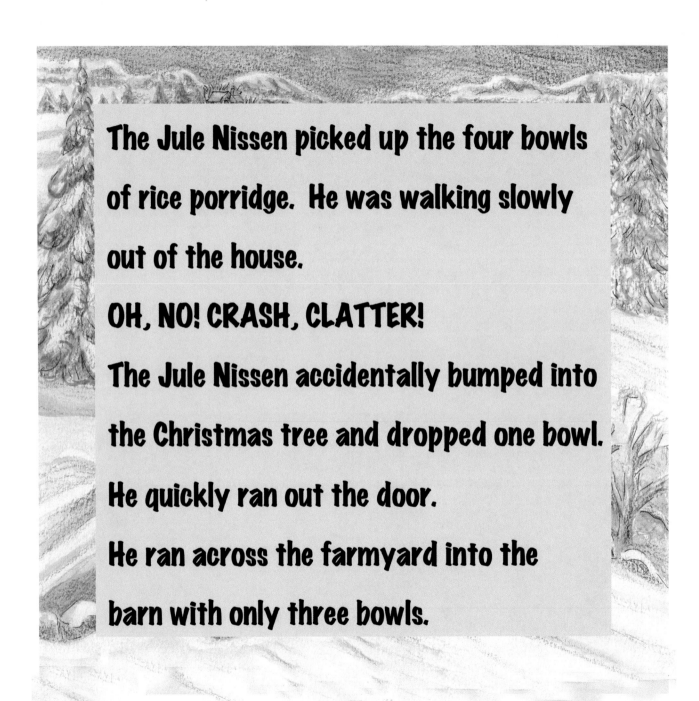

The Jule Nissen picked up the four bowls of rice porridge. He was walking slowly out of the house.

OH, NO! CRASH, CLATTER!

The Jule Nissen accidentally bumped into the Christmas tree and dropped one bowl.

He quickly ran out the door.

He ran across the farmyard into the barn with only three bowls.

The mother and father went into the living room. They saw the mess of porridge on the floor.

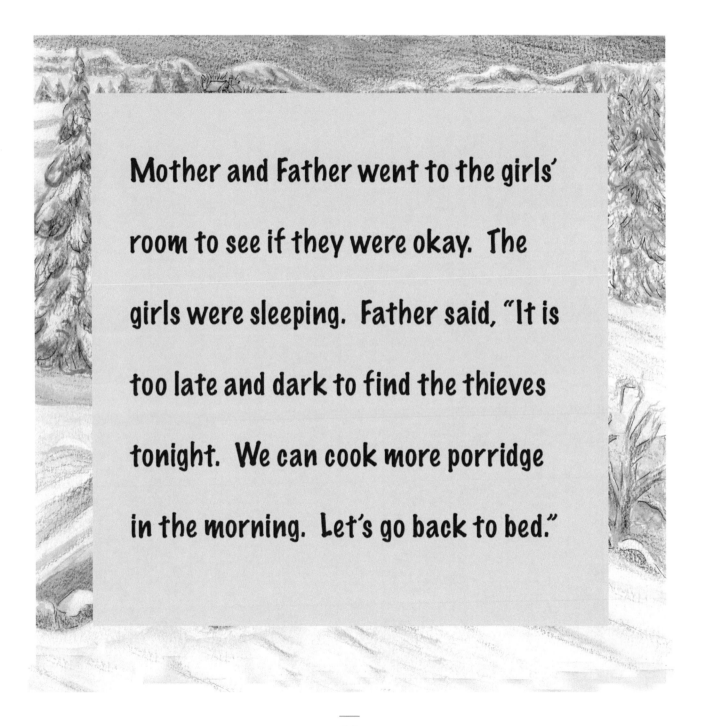

Mother and Father went to the girls' room to see if they were okay. The girls were sleeping. Father said, "It is too late and dark to find the thieves tonight. We can cook more porridge in the morning. Let's go back to bed."

The next morning the family went down for breakfast. Father said, "I saw four-toed footprints in the snow this morning. The four-toed Jule Nissen has been here. He is the one who stole the porridge. I believe he has taken it to the barn to feed the animals porridge on Christmas Day."

The farmer's wife was happy that the animals were happy. She decided that next year at Christmas (and all Christmases forevermore) she would make an extra pot of rice porridge for the Jule Nissen.

The farmer made a cart for the Jule Nissen to carry the porridge without an accident.

Daughter One said, "Let's call him the Farting Four-toed troll."

Mother said, "Yes, he did fart but he said, "Excuse me". Let's call him by his real name. Then he will not feel sad".

"Jule Nissen!"
"Christmas Troll!"

Jule calendar

A Jule calendar is the Norwegian word for a Christmas calendar. It is the same as an advent calendar. This one has the Jule Nissen (Christmas troll) feeding the cows.

Chest painted in Rosemaling

Rosemaling is a Norwegian decorative pattern of painting on wood using flowing flower ornamentation. Here it is with a Jule Nissen doll.

Wish a Norwegian a Merry Christmas by saying, "God Jul" (

A Norwegian tradition is to eat rice porridge at Christmas (Jul). There will be an almond in the porridge. If you are the lucky one to get the almond, you win a prize.

Rice Porridge (Risengrynsgrøt)

Boil about 2 ½ pints of milk. Add about 1 cup of rice slowly to the milk and let it simmer for about an hour. Add 1 teaspoon of salt. When it is the texture you like, put it in bowls. Add melted butter with cinnamon and sugar.

Norwegians eat another dish similar to rice porridge. It is called cream porridge (rømmegrøt). It is made with thick sour cream, milk, flour, and salt.

Thank you for purchasing this book. You can find more fun books by Lavelle Carlson at www.amazon,.com:

EEK! I Hear a Squeak
The Book of IF for Children
Can A Toucan Hoot Too? (storybook and coloring book)
Galapagos Rules! Postcards from Poppies
I Am Not Sleeping (storybook and coloring book)
Baby Bunny Bouncing
Dog Gone! Where Has My Dog Gone? (storybook/coloring book)

Made in the USA
Middletown, DE
22 July 2022

69612420R00020